LUCINA PRESS

SPRING, 2025

Book-Length Novel

Lucina Press, Centralia WA. www.lucinapress.com.
ISBN: 979-8-9927922-1-8
Copyright Sara Light-Waller, 2025. All rights reserved.
Cover artwork copyright Sara Light-Waller, 2025. All rights reserved.
Interior design copyright @2025, by Sara Light-Waller. All rights reserved.
Book design copyright @2025, by Sara Light-Waller. All rights reserved.

THE ORIGINAL MOON MAN

Frederick C. Davis' "Robin Hood in Glass"

THE "MOON MAN" was created by Frederick C. Davis. He appeared in thirty-eight novelettes from 1933 through 1938 in the pulp magazine, ***Ten Detective Aces***. The masked hero is the alter ego of Police Detective Sergeant Stephen Thatcher, son of the police chief, and best friend of the squad's ace detective, Gil McEwen. McEwen has vowed to send the Moon Man to the electric chair at all costs. Steve often admits quietly that he believes he'll do it, too. Steve is the fiancé of McEwen's daughter, Sue. About a quarter of the way into the series, Sue finds out that Steve is the Moon Man. Understanding that his mission — to steal from the corrupt and give the money to Great City's needy — is selfless, she helps him whenever she can. The Moon Man's true-hearted associate — Ned "Angel" Dargan — is his "ambassador extraordinaire" and he distributes the loot to the poor and needy. Because Steve's mask is a special helmet made of two-way glass, the character was nicknamed —"Robin Hood in glass."

The original run of stories was packed with built-in conflicts. If Steve's secret is ever discovered, it would devastate old Police Chief Thatcher, Steve's father, perhaps leading to a heart attack. The discovery would also bring anguish to Gil McEwen and Sue—who would lose the love of her life to the electric chair. Brave Ned Dargan is in the same boat as Thatcher as both share the same crimes — theft, kidnapping, and a bum murder rap.

I loved the original series. When I found out that the Moon Man was in the public domain, I had to try my hand at writing him. It is my honor and pleasure to pen this new Moon Man story in the spirit of Davis's pulp hero. I hope you enjoy reading "Shadow on the Moon" as much as I enjoyed writing it.

Sara Light-Waller
Centralia, WA
November 2025

The Great City Guardian

Vol. IV, NO. 25   GREAT CITY, MARCH 17, 1936   SINGLE COPIES FIVE CENTS

MOON MAN GIVES AID

Controversial Vigilante Keeps Poor Families Out of Hooverville After Devastating Fire

In the early hours of March 3rd, a tenement fire broke out on 35th Street in Midtown West. The broken-down gas heater that caused the blaze killed four, injured ten, and displaced thirty-five families. The buildings lacked fire escapes and while fire fighters struggled with frozen hydrants, two people leaped to their deaths. Two others later died of smoke inhalation. How many times has this happened in our city? Old buildings, poorly kept up by landlords, have caused nearly a dozen block fires in the past three years! The Department of Public Welfare is already overburdened. The displaced families—cold, hungry, and without hope—were destined to join Hooverville encampments in Central Park. Help, if it ever was to come from the city, would be too late. But help did come in time—from the Moon Man.

The masked vigilante known as the Moon Man is a controversial figure, no doubt. Claims about him vary widely. We have multiple accounts of a mysterious accomplice handing out packets of cash to the victims of the Midtown West fire. Several victims claimed this money kept them from starving. Another admitted it kept his family from a tar shack. One old grandmother, with faded eyes and a patched housedress under her ragged coat, praised the Moon Man effusively. "He's a good man—don't let anyone tell you different. Them coppers should leave him be!"

Others also praised his actions. The president of the Midtown chapter of the Benevolent and Protective Order of Elks, Laurence Sullivan, had this to say, "Vigilantism is everywhere nowadays. Mostly we see it against the commies, but this type of thing—the Moon Man, I mean — is something else again. Without his help, most of the displaced fire victims would have died. I don't like to say this, but I'm glad he did it! Not the thieving, I'm not for that. But the cause. I believe in that."

While Mayor Giardino has kept mum on the subject of Great City's popular vigilante, the police have not. According to Detective Lieutenant Gilbert McEwen, the Moon Man is an unrepentant murderer. Captain Peter Thatcher is more circumspect. "The Moon Man must be brought to justice. People refer to him as a Robin Hood figure, but he's still a criminal. We will catch him."

Is he a murderer? The District Attorney claims they have a case but won't go into details until the bandit is caught and put on trial.

We estimate funds given out by the Moon Man, or his accomplice, have saved the lives of dozens, if not hundreds, displaced persons in this city. While the Home Relief Bureau promises aid, their efforts are often delayed by weeks. What are victims supposed to do while they wait? Help from the Salvation Army can only go so far! Love him or hate him, the Moon Man is Great City's particular institution. We could do worse.

VIGILANTISM AND THE POOR

By Peter Thatcher
CAPTAIN OF POLICE, GREAT CITY

Vigilantism has been on the rise in cities across America. Many believe it is a conservative reaction to rising tides of socialism. As a policeman, it is not my place to share personal beliefs about either conservative or socialist movements. However, when these social groups collide in vigilante actions, it is the duty of the police to intercede on behalf of the ordinary citizen. Newsmen have accused us of looking the other way when masked vigilantes intercede in union struggles, especially when business owners have socialist sympathies. The reverse is true. Police do not consider vigilantism valid means of law enforcement, no matter the cause.

The past few years have been tough on everyone. Crooks have become more resourceful. Underworld gangs and racketeers have set their sights on bigger prizes. Some decent men, who have lost everything, find little incentive to keep to the straight and narrow. The policeman's task is immense and police work around the clock. Modern advances, such as new radio-cars, help us respond more promptly to calls for help. It is our job to keep the public safe and we do a good job at it. But the police need the support of the citizenry. Without their support, our task is much harder.

Take, for example, the masked vigilante known as the Moon Man. He has become a popular figure, stealing for the poor, like a modern-day Robin Hood. Many witnesses claim his stolen loot is handed out to the poor and disenfranchised. Despite these credible claims, the Moon Man is a criminal. Theft is not the best way to help. Side-stepping the law is no answer. Far better to look to the agencies set up for this purpose. That route may be slower, but it is the correct one.

The ordinary citizen wants stability in their lives, and the police work tirelessly to help them achieve it. Vigilantism hinders our efforts, especially when that vigilante has the approval of so many in Great City. The police will never approve of the Moon Man's activities, no matter what his stated goals. And we will bring him to justice, rest assured of that.

McEwen had a murderous gleam in his eyes. "You won't get away from me this time, you fancy crook!"

Shadow On The Moon

A New "Moon Man" Novella

By SARA LIGHT-WALLER

Author of "Landscape of Darkness," "Incorruptible," and "Battle at Neptune."

The sinister Nine Spheres use innocent citizens as unwitting thieves. This time they've set their sights on Sue McEwen, daughter of ace police detective, Gil McEwen and fiance of Steve Thatcher, secretly The Moon Man!.

CHAPTER 1

An expensive roadster, engine roaring and rear windshield cracked by a tearing bullet wound, speeded recklessly through the city. A few blocks behind, police sirens screamed. The driver, cheek torn by an ugly gash, veered off the main street and dashed for the river drive. The right sleeve of his coat was a torn mess and blood seeped darkly through the fabric. The car wove recklessly through the light evening traffic as sweat, mingled with blood, dripped down the driver's face. He was a portly man of middle age, face ghastly pale in the greenish glow of the dashboard lights. The man wiped a hand across his eyes and pressed the accelerator down hard. The roadster skidded around two cars on a side street as the sirens grew louder. The river was in sight now, as was the drive just before it. Heart beating a fast tattoo, he squealed around a corner and the roadster leaped onto the short street, which served as the entrance to the drive.

Colored lights, flashing hectically, appeared in the rear-view mirror. Three armored police cars hurtled closer. The driver pulled his roadster onto the drive and plunged north. There was no traffic on the East Side Drive at this hour and he pressed the peddle to the floor. The engine revved and the speedometer's needle rose towards ninety and then, faster still.

The police cars hurtled onto the drive in furious pursuit.

The roadster's driver glanced briefly into the rearview mirror and realized he couldn't outrun the cops for much longer. He glanced quickly across the front seat. A pretty girl sat slumped, unconscious, on the seat beside him. Her hands were tied behind her and there was a rag stuffed into her attractive mouth. On the floor near her feet was a satchel containing ten thousand dollars. He knew he could not fulfill his mission. He knew there was no escape for him. But the girl ... did she have to die with him? Suddenly, he couldn't stomach the thought. He turned the wheel hard onto the last exit before the drive opened up to the boroughs north of the city. He gambled that the police would be surprised and not catch him until he made his last defiant action against the Nine Spheres. The roadster turned hard, too fast, and skidded, squealing, onto two wheels. The driver fought the wheel and the car settled down. He flew down a side street, away from the drive. The police cars roared to follow.

On a small residential street, the driver risked another glance into the rearview mirror. He'd gained some ground and was now a few blocks ahead. He jerked to a stop and reached across the front seat, pushing open the passenger door. He shoved the girl hard. She rolled out of the car, bounced off the running board, then fell to the sidewalk in a folded heap. The fall jarred the girl awake, and she gasped behind the gag. He didn't bother to pull the door closed, just spirted away from the curb and pressed down the gas pedal as far as it would go. The pretty street was punctuated by venerable and sturdy trees. The man behind the wheel whispered something unintelligible and plunged towards an old oak. The crash made a tremendous and terrible sound. The girl struggled up onto one elbow and goggled. There was no question of the driver's survival.

The police roared up a moment later. The cars stopped at various angles on the narrow street. Out of one, a handsome young man came running. He sprinted to the girl's side and tore the gag from her mouth, the bonds from her wrists. His clean-cut face was deep-frowned with desperate worry. Sweat glistened on his brow. "Sue darling, are you alright?"

She slumped into his arms. "I'm fine, Steve," she whispered, then fainted.

Stephen Thatcher, Detective Sergeant of Great City's police force, paced his office while waiting for the staff doctor to finish checking over his fiancée, Sue McEwen. She maintained that she was fine, but Steve and her father, Gil McEwen, had insisted. Sue's kidnapping had hit him harder than it had Gil. Harder because he knew he was the cause.

Doctor Reinhold opened the door of the infirmary and looked out. Steve and Gil came bolting. The doctor said: "Best come in," and went back into the room.

Sue was sitting in a chair beside Reinhold's desk. She'd touched up her make-up and was putting on lipstick as the two men stepped into the room. Sue capped the lipstick, then clasped the tiny mirror in her hand shut. She looked up at Steve and, despite her smile, he could see the tension in her eyes and at the corners of her lovely mouth.

"How is she?" McEwen demanded. His steely gray eyes were harsh with worry.

"I've taken a sample of Miss McEwen's blood. We won't know for sure until I get it back from the lab. Until then, I suggest she go home and rest."

"How long before you get the results?" Steve demanded. He took Sue's hand.

"Tomorrow morning, most likely."

Steve's jaw clenched. "And if it's positive for the drug?"

"There is an antidote but I can't give it to her until we're sure. Until then she must not be allowed to leave our sight."

Sue's small hand trembled in Steve's. She glanced up at him, expression pained.

"Sue, darling, did they give you anything? Do you remember?" He asked, worriedly.

"I don't think they did. All I remember is that they took me somewhere, an apartment with the drapes drawn. I did see two of the Nine Spheres; one was tall and broad, and the other shorter. I think the short man was the boss of the two. At least he was giving orders."

"Did you hear them mention anything about their meeting place?" McEwen asked.

"No, Dad. That man who was killed ... who was he?"

"A businessman from Astoria named Sal Merton. His shop sells hardware and paint. By damn! This racket uses ordinary citizens for their leg men. It's crazy!" Gil McEwen, hardened detective, nemesis of lawbreakers, chomped his unlighted cigar and looked at his daughter appraisingly. "If they did give you that drug, Sue, we know they'll call you on the phone and order you to do something. And you'll obey without a thought."

Sue clasped the purse in her lap with stiffened fingers. "Yes," she said quietly.

"Then we must keep her away from the phone," Steve snapped. "We'll have someone stay with her at all times."

Sue's glance drifted downwards, hiding the anxious look in her eyes. "I'll be alright. Once we know about the drug—"

"Until we do, I'm not letting you out of my sight," Steve declared.

"Sue, can you remember anything else about where they took you?" McEwen asked, tensely.

She'd been snatched from a Lowell's Department Store while shopping. It had been the strangest thing—she'd been in the perfume aisle making a purchase when a distressed middle-aged matron grabbed her elbow and steered her towards the changing rooms in the back, insisting that a woman was in need of help. Sue quickly discovered there was no other woman, instead a man with a cloth soaked in chloroform waiting for her in the changing rooms.

When she came to, she was in the apartment with two men, tied up on the sofa. Each man wore a dark mask that covered his entire face. On the upper cheek of the left side, stylized stars were picked out in silver paint. Those blank mask faces were strangely eerie, giving no hint of any expression. They told her they were part of the Nine Spheres and she was being held for ransom. If the money was delivered, she would not be harmed. They called McEwen and demanded ten thousand dollars for his daughter's safe return.

McEwen had agreed to pay it and was given instructions as to where and when to make the drop. Sue heard this conversation on the phone. She waited in the apartment as the men went in and out a few times. She'd tried to chivvy her hands loose from the knots, but they were too tight. "I must have fallen asleep while we were waiting," she confessed. "The next thing I knew, I was pushed out of that car. I fell onto the sidewalk ... and then that horrible crash..." She flinched visibly and a small, pained gasp escaped her lips as the bleak memories returned to her.

"So they could have given you something..." Steve prompted.

"Maybe, I don't...remember." Sue looked up at him with frightened eyes.

In an executive office in the upper stories of the Bingo Tires Company, a short man in glasses and an eye shade sat at a desk with a large sheet of vellum spread before him. A desk lamp illuminated a circular drawing covering almost the entire sheet. The circular design was scattered with arcane symbols in either red or blue pencil. The man adjusted his eyeglasses then picked up a metal straightedge. He laid it across the drawing, making an angle with another line marked in blue. He picked up a red pencil and traced the new line. Then he picked up a pamphlet and thumbed through it. His finger traced down a column of figures and stopped at a particular line. He glanced at the pocket watch laying open on the desk before him. Another glance at the column of figures and he nodded slightly. Picking up the blue pencil again, he marked another sigil on the circular drawing then studied it for a moment. He picked up the phone. "Operator, connect me to number ALS-223." A moment later, he was connected.

A gravelly voice on the other end of the line said: "This is Mars."

"Mars, this is Mercury. We have a problem. Our new talent is being interfered with. Shadow her and if you can get things rolling, do so. She's at Police Headquarters."

"Can't we use the regular methods?" Mars asked.

Mercury consulted the chart again. "No. That's odd; apparently we're having interference from Luna. You're his contact. Where is he?"

"I haven't seen him for a couple of days," Mars answered gruffly. "I'll find out. Do you think he's double crossing us?"

"I don't see why he would; he's as deep into this as we are. Find out and let me know."

Mars hung up the phone and dragged a scarred hand across his chin. "That little weasel," he muttered while pulling on his overcoat. He mashed a homburg down onto his close-cropped hair then slipped from his rented room. Mars tramped down the house stairs and out into the cold night. His breath plumed as he walked. A few blocks later, the neighborhood changed. The blue collar boarding houses were replaced by

bars and taxi-dancers. He passed a movie theater with a flashing marquis. The next block had apartments over the shops. Midway down the block was an optometrist's shop. He stopped before the door to the left of the shop's entrance and pressed a buzzer. A pleasant male voice answered. "Yes, who is it?"

"Mars," came the gruff reply. "I want to talk to you."

A buzzer sounded and the door unlocked.

Upstairs, a dapper man wearing an eye shade opened the door. "Come in, quickly." He ushered the much larger man inside, then shut the door. He gestured at a table covered with tidy stacks of cash. "You're early. I'm just getting the loot ready now."

"Mercury said that you've been interfering with the new pigeon. What gives?"

The man, whose code name was Luna, pointed a thin finger at his own chest. "Me? You're crazy."

"He read the chart, he knows." His voice held a slight inflection indicating awe.

"I've done nothing of the kind, I tell you!" Luna insisted. "There's the loot from the last heist. Count it if you want. Go on..." He narrowed his eyes at Mars belligerently.

Mars strode to the table and did a quick and dirty tally. "Yeah, this looks alright. Okay. But Mercury knows...if it wasn't you interfering..."

Luna rolled his eyes. "Must be some other slob. Hey, wait a minute." Behind his cheaters, his eyes lit. "Luna is another way of talking about the moon. Maybe the interference is coming from someone else using the moon moniker."

Mars' brutal mouth stiffened. "The Moon Man."

Luna's face became momentarily rigid with dread. "You get out of here and tell Mercury that!"

Gil McEwen's heels beat against the floorboards as he paced the infirmary. His jaw was clenched around his cigar. After a moment he declared: "We have the ransom money in the safe here at headquarters. If they did drug Sue, they might ask her to bring it to them. We'll keep an eye on her here, where there are plenty of people to watch out for her."

"And if they did drug her?" Steve snapped. "Doctor, what can we do about that? Is there an antidote?"

Doctor Reinhold shuffled through some papers on his desk. He pulled out a singular sheet and glanced at it. "Merton's autopsy showed traces of a *Datura stramonium* derivative in his system."

"Poison!" McEwen exclaimed, horrified.

The doctor looked grim. "Datura is a toxic plant, but there are people who use it to create visions for ritual purposes. Whoever created this drug for the Nine Spheres knew all about how to use it for something other than murder."

"Where would they get it?" Steve asked.

"The plant grows wild in the Southwestern United States and in Mexico. It wouldn't be hard to find."

"Dad," Sue said suddenly, "there's something I'd forgotten until just now. The tall man called the shorter, Mercury."

Steve wracked his brains for any crook he was aware by the name of Mercury. He could think of none and said so.

"Let's check the files," McEwen said. "I don't recall any either. Sue, you stay here with the doctor."

After twenty minutes they'd came up empty. There was no one on the books with that name, or alias. But there was a pile of connected crime reports on McEwen's desk. In each case, the crime had been committed by an ordinary city resident with no prior criminal history. In each case, the thief had died after stealing a large sum of money, jewels, or bonds. Each death had been different, all self-inflicted. The loot was never recovered, only the dead thief, who had

never been a crook before. The only exception was the money Gil McEwen had borrowed from the city for Sue's ransom.

Steve left the file room and went to his office. He closed the door, then took a folded scrap of paper from his vest pocket. He unfolded the paper and smoothed it flat on the desk. There were odd symbols written on it: circles, half-moons, straight lines, and crosses. It wasn't a language, but the symbols were consistent and seemed to create a message if you knew how to read them. Unfortunately, he didn't. He made a grim mouth as he re-folded the paper and put it back into his pocket. He walked back down the hall to the infirmary.

Sue was standing, looking out the window at the cityscape beyond. She turned as Steve came in. The girl smiled for his sake, although it was obviously forced. "Darling, I'd like to go home. I'm very tired."

Steve smiled ruefully. "I don't doubt it, but we can't leave you alone tonight. Gil will be here for hours yet, and I have to go out for a little while. It'd be best if you stay here. There's a cot in the back of the card room where you can lie down."

Sue nodded wearily, her smile fading. "Yes, of course. I suppose that must do." Then her gaze became thoughtful. She looked at Steve searchingly and said: "I'd like to come with you, if you'll let me. Then you'll have no trouble keeping an eye on me."

"Alright. I shouldn't be gone for too long, anyway."

She put on her impertinent little hat and he helped her on with her coat. Sue snugged her arm through his.

Doctor Reinhold said: "Steve, if she shows any symptoms you must bring her back immediately."

Sue paled. "What kind of symptoms, Doctor?"

"That's the trouble," he admitted. "I'm not sure."

"You'll tell me if you feel anything ... odd, won't you, Sue?" Steve asked, concernedly. His worried glance traveled over her pretty face, looking for a sign that she was unwell.

Sue smiled back confidently, then reached up and kissed him. "I'm fine, darling. Don't worry. I promise to tell you the moment I feel anything out of the ordinary. Let's tell Dad I'm going with you."

Outside in the evening chill, Sue shivered inside her coat. She glanced up at the moon, just rising above the city lights. "Where are we going?"

Steve helped her into his roadster. "To see a fortune-teller."

"Why?"

He got behind the wheel and powered the engine. As the car spurted away from the curb, he said: "the Moon Man was planning a robbery the night you were kidnapped. At the same department store, as a matter of fact. The owner, Sandy Lowell, is a notorious gambler and uses his department store to launder money. I planned to rob the store and give the money to the people whose homes were burned out last week in the Rose Hill fire. Social Services hasn't the money to help them and they have nothing. That crooked money was going to help them. Sue, the Moon Man was there when you were kidnapped. Had I known ... I would have...." His voice was bitter. "I won't let them hurt you, I promise you that." He looked grimly at the road ahead, mouth set and taut.

"Steve, you couldn't have known."

They were driving towards the west side of the city, to an area consisting of mainly residential apartments but also a few small shops. "I was there the next day, looking for clues. I found a slip of paper near the ladies' changing rooms. On it were strange symbols. I have an idea of what they mean, but I want to be sure." The roadster pulled to a stop outside a shop whose picture window was decorated with three neon-glowing signs. They read: "Madame Mystery" and "Futures Foretold." To one side was a large, stylized hand, palm facing outwards.

Despite the late hour, the shop was open and Steve escorted Sue inside. A jangling bell announced their entrance into the sweet-smelling shop. Some exotic incense was burning from joss sticks in wooden holders on a table. The place was dimly lighted by small lamps with colored glass shades. The anteroom was empty except for a few shopworn chairs, a small table, and three sickly-looking potted palms. A dark curtain with silver stars marked the passageway into another room. The walls of the waiting room were adorned with charts filled with symbols similar to those on the note in Steve's pocket.

"Hello?" Steve called.

The spangled curtain pulled aside and an elderly woman shuffled through. She was tall but stooped with age and leaning on a cane. The old woman was dressed in a gypsy's get-up, complete with beaded shawl.

"I am Madame Mystery. How can I help you?" She gazed at the young couple with frank appraisal.

Steven took the slip of paper from his vest pocket and unfolded it. "I'd like you to take a look at this and see if you can tell me what it says." He held the slip out towards the fortune teller.

Madame Mystery shuffled forwards and took the paper from him. She walked closer to one of the lamps, smoothed the paper flat on the table and squinted at it. After a moment, her head shot up. "Where did you get this?" she demanded.

"Never mind that. What does it say?"

"Take it away," she insisted, holding the paper out with a tremulous hand. "I want no part in the Nine Spheres' schemes!" Her whiskery upper lip trembled.

"If you know what it says, you must tell me," Steve insisted. "This girl's life is in danger."

Madame Mystery's hand tightened around the handle of her cane. She walked to the front door and locked it. Then returned to the curtained doorway from which she had appeared. "Come into the back with me."

The back room was better lighted than the antechamber. It had three chairs surrounding a round table covered by a scarlet cloth. A crystal ball stood shining on a stand in the center of the table. "Sit down." The gypsy spread out Steve's symbol-covered paper before her, then waited until the two were seated before speaking again. "These symbols are the language of astrology. This paper is a horoscope, a map of the stars at a certain time."

"And you can read it..." Steve said. "What does it say? Tell me!"

The old woman glanced again at the paper. "The date for this horoscope was two days ago. The place is here in the city, the time ... about 3:30 in the afternoon."

"How do you know the Nine Spheres had anything to do with it?" Sue asked quietly.

The old woman's finger pointed to the upper left section of the glyphs. "Here, a conjunction between Jupiter and Pluto. And here, a sextile between Saturn and Neptune. This paper is the horoscope for a crime. I have heard that the Nine Spheres use these methods to discern the best time for their robberies."

"Does it say anything else about ... the crime?" Sue asked.

The old woman shook her head. "The time has passed for this crime. This horoscope is over; it no longer has any power. Except..." She looked down at the paper again.

"Well!" Steve snapped. "What else does it say?"

When the old woman looked up, her eyes were shadowed with deep fear. "This part here says to beware the moon tonight as it heralds unexpected surprises."

Sue clutched Steve's arm. He rested a hand atop her own, glancing at her briefly before turning back to the fortune-teller. "Thank you. How much do I owe you for your time?"

Madame Mystery opened her mouth to speak, but then stopped. She stared at Steve for a long moment, then shook her head. "You already do enough for this city. You owe me nothing."

Steve's heart pounded in his chest. Did this old gypsy somehow know he was a policeman, or was it something else? Did she know he was also the Moon Man?

Sue was gazing intently at one of the strange circular diagrams on the wall. Her eyes drifted from one diagram to another. Suddenly, her features froze, expression becoming strange and distant. She stood up, jerkily, then pointed at the old fortune-teller with a stiffened finger. Sue's expression was one of downright hostility, even hatred. "One of the moon's surprises awaits you, old woman," she said in a strange and uncanny voice. "You should not have interfered."

The old woman's head snapped up and she frowned at Sue in perplexity. Sue laughed, a hollow sound laced with cruelty. Madame Mystery's eyes flew wide and she trembled, wizened face draining of color until it was the hue of faded paper. She pushed back from the table and lurched unsteadily to her feet. "Get ... get out of here!"

Steve stared at Sue, but it was like looking at a stranger. There was something about her face; she seemed an entirely different person.

Sue stepped towards the old gypsy woman. The cold cruelty of her expression chilled Steve to the bone. He grabbed her arm, restraining her. "Sue?"

Sue's callous expression drained away and her tense body relaxed. She looked around in obvious confusion. Her eyes lit on the terrified old woman and she stared as if she'd never seen her before. "What happened...?"

"I told you to get out of here!" the old woman shrieked. "Go now!"

"What happened...?" Sue repeated, muzzily. "Steve, I don't understand...." He felt her tremble in reaction.

Steve put a hand on her elbow and directed her firmly towards the door of the shop. The girl was initially resistant, but soon acquiesced. "It'll be alright, Sue. Come on."

Before they passed through the spangled curtain, Sue paused to look back at the old gypsy. Madame Mystery stood with her back to the wall, looking terrified.

Sue swallowed, bit her lower lip, then hurried through the curtain.

CHAPTER 2

As the roadster sped away from the fortune-teller's shop, Sue wrung her hands. "But I don't remember saying anything like that, Steve!" Her hands clenched around the purse in her lap.

"What do you remember, darling?"

"Well, I ... I guess I was looking at one of those strange charts on the wall. She said something odd to you, didn't she? I can't quite recall what it was. Then ... she was angry with me and frightened. That's all I can remember, honestly."

Steve's brow furrowed. Police Headquarters was busy. What if Sue had another episode? She could easily slip out without anyone being the wiser. Until they were sure what the drug in her system was, there could be no antidote for her. Until then, someone needed to watch her every moment. He turned a corner and headed the car in a new direction.

"The Moon Man? That could be messy. I'll contact Neptune. Miss McEwen was his suggestion. He can damn well clean up his own mess!" Mercury, in reality, Sampson Stark, owner of Bingo Tires, hung up the phone and considered. The Nine Spheres association was his idea and so far it had been plenty profitable. Certainly more than his own failing tire company. A few more jobs and they'd go their separate ways, rich men.

Mercury didn't like clutter; he liked things to go smoothly. Sandy Lowell—Neptune—was an opportunist. When he noticed Sue McEwen frequenting his department store, he suggested she be their next target. They'd grabbed her and injected her with the datura derivative, just like all the others. Had things gone to plan, a simple phone call would have activated her. Now she was who-knows-where and maybe the Moon Man was also involved. "I don't like it," Mercury muttered to himself. "With the datura in her system, she'll start hallucinating. And without our guidance..." His expression hardened. "She's going to fixate on something else."

The middle class neighborhood was quiet, families long abed. Steve drove to an unassuming bungalow and parked out front. "Stay here a moment," he said and got out of the car. He walked to the garage and pulled the door open. A familiar roadster was parked inside. At his beckoning gesture, Sue got out of the car. Steve closed the garage door as she walked forward to meet him. Together, they hurried up the short walk to the front door. Steve fitted a key into the lock and pushed the door open. Inside, the house was dark. He turned on a lamp and then went to the bottom of the stairs. He called up: "Angel!"

A stocky man wearing pajamas came down the steps with a revolver held securely in one fist. When the ex-pug recognized them, his anxiety evaporated. He lowered the gat. "Boss! Sue! What are you doing here?"

"I need your help, Angel." Steve directed Sue towards an armchair and she slumped into it, wearily. Her color was poor—tired and sallow. She barely noticed Dargan's presence.

In all the world only Ned "Angel" Dargan and Sue McEwen knew the Moon Man's true identity. The masked vigilante had once saved Dargan from sickness and starvation. Now he was the Moon Man's trusted accomplice and ambassador extraordinaire. The ex-pug with the battered nose and cauliflower ear glanced over at Sue worriedly then turned back to Steve with a question in his eyes.

"Angel, I need you to watch her for me." He explained about the kidnapping and the datura in Sue's system. "Do not let her speak to anyone on the phone—even me, understand?"

"Sure, Boss. What can we do for her? She doesn't look so good."

Sue was collapsed now, lolling half-conscious in the armchair. Her eyes were closed and her head drooped slightly, tilted back against the cushions. Steve felt a light sweat break out on his forehead. She must get an antidote before something terrible happened! But that couldn't happen until the toxicology report came back ... hours yet! "Try to keep her comfortable. I'll call you as soon as I have some answers."

Dargan's eyes traveled to the telephone on the desk, then returned to Steve.

"Do not let her answer the phone," Steve repeated harshly. He went to Sue and touched her cheek. "Sue dear, can you hear me?"

Her eyelids fluttered. "Steve?"

"I'm leaving you with Angel for a while. Try and rest. I'll be back soon."

She nodded wearily, then suddenly bolted upright, eyes white. She trembled visibly, as if shocked. "The moon! The moon!" she moaned. "Beware! There's a shadow on the moon!" Then her eyes rolled up in her head and she sagged against the back of the chair, unconscious.

Dargan stared at her, shocked. "God, Boss! Are you sure we shouldn't take her to the hospital right now?"

Steve groaned and shook his head. "Not unless we have to." He picked up the phone's receiver and dialed a familiar number—Police Headquarters. He told the switchboard operator he wanted to speak with Doctor Reinhold and was put through immediately. "Doctor, this is Steve Thatcher. Any word back on Sue's blood test?"

"Nothing yet, Steve. I'm sorry."

Steve glanced at the girl passed out in the armchair. "I have Sue with me. She's had a couple of ... episodes." He described them, only giving the broad outlines of the strange events at Madame Mystery's shop.

"What you describe could be datura poisoning," Reinhold said, voice grim. "Is there somewhere she can rest while under supervision?"

"I have someone watching her now, and she's asleep."

"That's the best thing for her. Keep her calm and free of external stimuli, if possible. It's after nine, we should hear something by morning."

"Thanks, Doc." Steve hung up the instrument and let go a held breath. "Watch her for me, Angel. I'll check in with you as soon as I can." Steve walked out of the bungalow without looking back. He slipped behind the wheel of his roadster and kicked the motor into gear. As the car rolled away from the curb, he thought about what the old gypsy had said—that tonight's moon heralded the unexpected. *So be it*, he thought. *But let that surprise come for the Nine Spheres!*

The Nine Spheres first appeared in Great City five months before. At first, their name wasn't known. It was only after the third robbery—a jewelry store heist—that they claimed the crime as their own. The actual theft was committed by the building's janitor, a man with no criminal record. He broke into the store and stole half a million in jewels. He left an enigmatic note on the glass counter, explaining that the music of the spheres had told him to steal the jewelry. The man was caught the next day, but there was no sign of the jewels. He seemed confused about the whole thing; he didn't deny committing the robbery but had no idea where the gemstones were. Even under harsh interrogation, he maintained he didn't know. The janitor's fingerprints were all over the crime scene, and that was enough to convict him for the theft. He was put in jail pending trial. They found him hanging from the rafters by his own belt the next morning.

The Nine Spheres' next victim was a fat, middle-aged priest. He robbed a bank at gunpoint. At first, the teller thought it was a joke; he simply couldn't believe a priest was holding him up. But the cleric meant business. Before leaving the bank, he shot a man who tried to wrestle him to the ground. Fortunately, the man was not killed. A squad car picked up the priest two hours later. By then, he was in such a state of remorse he begged to be arrested. There was no sign of the cash. The priest was released on bail paid by the local parish. He overdosed on sleeping pills that night.

Three more robberies followed. All of them committed by ordinary citizens who later claimed not to understand why they'd done it. In all cases, the loot was gone. In every case, the thief killed himself within two days after the crime had been committed.

Sue was meant to be the next victim. This was the first time the Nine Spheres had asked for ransom. Gil McEwen had borrowed the money from city coffers, vowing the kidnappers would never get it. And now the money was back in police hands. But the bagman for the ransom money was dead and Sue was under the influence of a strange drug. The only clue Steve had was a slip of paper with a horoscope for the kidnapping's day and time. Perhaps that wasn't the only mistake the Nine Spheres had made that night. He needed to find out.

The car sped across town to Lowell's Department Store. At this late hour the edifice was dark, the front display windows black as the devil's own hollow eyes. Steve pulled the roadster into the alley beside the store. Blank brick surrounded a single side door. He stepped from the roadster and glanced around. The alley was empty. Steve unlocked the rumble compartment and pulled out a case. Inside was a dark robe wrapped around a spherical object slightly larger than a man's head. Carefully, and with ears alert to any sound, he unwrapped the uncanny sphere. Under the moonlight it gleamed silver. He momentarily returned the fragile sphere to the case, then shrugged the black robe over his strong, young shoulders. He pulled a pair of black gloves from the case and drew them on over his hands. With delicate care, he picked up the silvered globe and flicked the catches separating it into two hemispheres. He placed the globe over his head and fixed it shut. Steve Thatcher, police detective was gone. And in his place, the most infamous of thieves, the Moon Man! He returned the case to the rumble, locking it securely. The Moon Man's dark robe melded into the colors of the night while the mirrored glass sphere seemed to float in the air, companion to the larger orb riding the heavens above the city's great towers.

The Moon Man glided to the department store's side door. He moved with absolute certainty despite the silvery globe atop his shoulders. The mirrored glass sphere, strange trademark of the Moon Man, was no hindrance to his sight. It was made of rare, one-way Argus glass. From the outside it appeared mirrored, except for the surface mottling which made it look like the face of the full moon. But looking outwards it afforded a view as clear as the finest cut crystal.

The department store's side entrance was locked, but this proved no barrier to the Moon Man. From a pocket beneath his robe he brought forth a packet of skeleton keys. Patiently, he tried one key, then another. The third key turned the lock. After another quick glance up and down the alley, he stepped inside. From his last failed attempt at robbery here, he knew the layout of the place well. Silently, he glided to the area where Sue had been kidnapped; the ladies' changing rooms. Taking a penlight from his pocket, he flashed the narrow beam around the darkened rooms. The light reflected off a small forgotten object under the edge of one changing room curtain. He reached down and his gloved fingers closed around a small rectangular object—a matchbox. It was an advertisement for Bingo Tires. On the box's cover, beside the blocky letters, was the company's logo—a sitting dog wearing a rilled collar. He shook the box and something rattled that didn't sound like matches. Pushing the box open, he saw a tiny gold lapel pin. Closing it again, he stuffed the matchbook into his pocket and continued the search. Suddenly, he heard approaching footsteps. A security guard! The Moon Man flicked off the penlight and ducked into one of the curtained changing rooms. The guard began checking each dressing room in turn. There were four of them and the Moon Man was in the last one in line. When the guard pulled open the curtains he let out a harsh cry of astonishment as his face was met with a hard fist. The startled guard crashed to the floor.

The Moon Man dragged the unconscious watchman into a booth. He tied his hands and feet with a curtain sash and shoved a handkerchief from one of the display racks into his mouth. The night phantom closed the alcove's curtains, then glided to a tiny elevator with a placard reading: "Employees Only." Stepping inside, he pressed a button. On the top floor was Sandy Lowell's office. Quietly, he unlocked the office door with the same skeleton key he'd used two nights before. Treading silently into the modernistic office, he flashed a beam of light at the desk. A quirk of a smile appeared on his lips. It was as he'd remembered. On one side of the desk was a thin volume with a gold printed title — "Ephemeris for 1936." He flipped it open and noted a series of numbers written in tidy pencil marks on the title page. Interspersed with these were some of the strange symbols he'd seen on the walls of Madame Mystery's shop. Flipping through the pages, he saw complex charts and tables using the same symbols. Snapping it shut, he slipped the small book into his pocket and glided to the safe, bulking in one corner of the room. The Moon Man, superb safe-cracker that he was, spun the dial and listened. After a few scant moments, he pulled the door open. Inside were the riches he'd planned to steal two days before—twenty thousand dollars in neatly stacked bills. A small pile of ledgers sat on a shelf above the money. He flipped the top one open. The now familiar symbology stared back at him from under the flashlight's beam. It was a journal of some kind, with dates marking each page. One symbol repeated itself too often for coincidence—two concave lines facing away from each other, with a line bifurcating the centers. His gaze settled on a short passage under the header from the day Sue was kidnapped. Beneath the words was another circular chart, with many symbols clustered into two sections of the segmented circle. Underneath, a scrawled note: *"The aspects look good for tomorrow at 3:30. Call Mars."*

The Moon Man's breath quickened—it was a note about Sue's kidnapping! He stuffed the notebooks into his pocket with the ephemeris. His gaze returned to the pile of cash. A feeling of dislocation came over him. His hand reached into his pocket and the gloved fingers brushed the valuable notebooks that could be the key to finding the mysterious Nine Spheres. But the money...all those people who'd lost their homes in the fire last week, they were suffering—homeless and with nothing. With grim resolve, he pulled out the stacks of cash and stuffed them into a cloth bag neatly folded on the lowest shelf. He shut the safe and spun the dial. As he glided from Lowell's office, the Moon Man heard the distant shriek of police sirens. He hurried to a window overlooking the street. Two police cars were just coming into view, lights flashing hectically. The Moon Man bypassed the small elevator in favor of the stairs. He'd have to find another way out of the building.

The security guard returned to consciousness and found himself trussed up like a Christmas turkey. He squirmed unsuccessfully, unable to free himself. But then he remembered the new alarm system just installed a few days before. There was a small box on the wall with a clock and push-button. If he didn't press the button every hour and a half, the time it took to make a complete circuit of the store, an alarm would go off at Police Headquarters. He knew he'd missed his last check-in. He also knew that the Moon Man was probably still in the building. He smirked behind his gag as he realized the police must be on their way.

The Moon Man surged up the stairs. Outside the building, the wailing sirens drew nearer. He reached the building's attic space and pushed open the doors. Glancing around quickly, he looked for an exit to the roof. Through the front windows, he saw colored lights flashing from below. Two patrol cars pulled up in front of the building. A pair of policemen got out of one car and out of the other ... McEwen! The steely-eyed manhunter was yelling orders which the Moon Man could not hear from the attic, but he had a pretty good idea by gestures of what McEwen was ordering his men to do.

Feverishly, the Moon Man glanced about. The attic was filled with open boxes of goods, holiday decor, and other things the shop might need occasionally. Across the space he saw a window overlooking the alley where his roadster was parked—Steve Thatcher's roadster! There was a fire escape leading down to the alley. As he watched, a blue-coated policeman walked around the corner and into the alley. Under his silvered helmet, the Moon Man felt his mouth go dry.

Gil McEwen raced through the department store with two policemen at his heels. The new alarm system had worked perfectly, alerting them to the robbery. The store owner, Sandy Lowell, had also been alerted at his home. Lowell had called Police Headquarters immediately and screamed bloody murder. His store had been robbed twice in one week! Aged Chief Thatcher, Steve Thatcher's father, assured Lowell they'd catch the thief. That was a promise. Which was why Police Detective Lieutenant Gil McEwen, nominally in charge of the department, had gone out to oversee the arrest. They found the security guard tied up on the floor of one of the ladies' changing rooms.

"It's the Moon Man!" the man gasped as the gag was pulled from his mouth.

McEwen's face became a grim mask, eyes chips of gray flint. "By damn, we have that fancy crook now! He's in here somewhere; we're going to get him this time!" One of the patrolmen untied the security guard while McEwen began a furious search.

In the alleyway, patrolman Tom Quincy chanced to look up and saw a flash of silver moving quickly across the roof.

He tore the side door open and pelted into the store. "Lieutenant! I saw him, the Moon Man! He's up on the roof!"

McEwen grabbed the security guard by the arm and demanded: "What's the fastest way to the roof?"

"Through the attic. It's this way."

McEwen, face hard with grim purpose, gestured to his men. "Quincy, you and Bartlett go outside and watch the fire escapes. Unless he's grown wings, he's not getting down any other way." The two patrolmen hurried out, one to the front of the building, the other to the side alley.

McEwen, the security guard, and the remaining policemen pelted to the staircase. McEwen had a murderous gleam in his eyes. "You won't get away this time," he swore through clenched teeth while mounting the stairs.

In the attic, they rushed to an opened window. Leaning out into the moonlit darkness, McEwen saw a gleam of silver sparkling over the lip of the roof. There was a fixed metal ladder attached to the side of the building outside the window. McEwen surged up the ladder, teeth clamped around his cigar. The patrolman and the guard followed. McEwen swung up onto the flat roof and saw something silvery flash in the

darkness. The silvery sphere was moving rapidly away, toward one of the chimneys. A ripple of black cloth trailed breezily beneath it. The detective bolted across the roof as the phantom came close to a chimney, then paused. "Got you now," McEwen muttered, grabbing for the trailing black cloth. The cloth pulled free in his hand and the silver globe fell, bouncing then breaking apart. McEwen bent to look. A dummy's head had been wrapped in a silver scarf. He swore. A dark dress had been pinned to a clothes line, the dummy's head fixed above it. He shook the dummy's head at the security guard, scowling ferociously. "What's wrong with this picture? Was he here or wasn't he?"

"I saw him!" The security guard insisted. "I did!"

In the alley below, patrolman Quincy was watching the fire escape while listening to McEwen's exclamations of fury, audible even on the street below. For this reason, he did not notice a quiet figure with a wrapped bundle under his arm slip around the side of the building and into the alleyway. The figure hurried to the parked roadster and unlocked the rumble compartment. Quickly, he shoved a black-wrapped bundle inside. This was followed by a full cloth bag and a stack of ledgers. Closing the compartment, he turned the key in the lock and then sauntered closer to Patrolman Quincy. Steve Thatcher whistled, apparently in amazement. The policeman turned at the sound and immediately recognized the clean-cut young man. "Steve! When did you get here?"

"A few minutes ago. I heard about the alarm on my car radio. No Moon Man, huh?"

Quincy grimaced. "Apparently not."

Steve Thatcher opened the side door of the building, the one he'd unlocked just a few minutes earlier, and walked in. He met McEwen in Sandy Lowell's burgled office. The ace detective was stewing, teeth clamped around his unlit cigar. McEwen commented sourly: "By damn, he's slipped us again, Steve!" Then his keen eyes widened in alarm. "Steve, where's Sue? Is she alright?"

"She's fine, Gil. I have a friend watching her. She's had strange visions; I think Doc may be right about datura poisoning."

"Oh God." McEwen turned away from Steve, shoulders slightly hunched under his coat.

"I've been working on the Nine Spheres angle," Steve said quietly. "So far, not much luck."

"We haven't found much either," McEwen admitted, turning back. "I've got a hunch that between their name and the use of a drug, they have some sort of occult connection."

"I agree." Steve's eyes scanned the office. He could see no other obvious occult symbology, but there was a telescope on a stand near one of the big windows. Steve uncapped it and looked through. "Gil, have a look at this."

McEwen strolled over, rubbing his five o'clock shadow. "You couldn't see the stars from here," he exclaimed. "There's too much city light."

"It's not pointed at the sky, anyway. See there, it's pointed right at the top floor of the building across the street." Steve's eyes fixated on the building's larger-than-life lighted sign of a sitting dog with a rilled collar. "That's the Bingo Tires building."

"So?" Gil said. "What's the connection?"

Steve shook his head slowly, all the while thinking about the fallen matchbox containing a gold lapel pin. "Gil, do you know who owns Bingo Tires? It's Sampson Stark."

McEwen peered through the telescope again and this time looked carefully. "It's hard to tell in the dark, but I think it's looking into an office. Could be Stark's office for all I know. Why would Sandy Lowell play Peeping Tom with Stark's building?" He rubbed his stubbly chin. "When I'm done here, I'm going to ask Lowell directly."

Steve glanced at the desk clock; its glowing dial read 9:30. "I'd rather Sue stay where she is tonight, Gil. She was sleeping when I left and, with any luck, she'll sleep through the night. I'll keep an eye on her and bring her with me to the station in the morning."

"Alright, Steve. I'll be at headquarters, call me if anything happens." Although he was putting up his usual tough front, Sue's condition lay heavily on Gil's mind. His relentless drive to capture the Moon Man was overshadowed for once by concerns for his daughter's safety.

Steve rested a hand on McEwen's shoulder. "She'll be okay, Gil. We'll get that antidote into her and she'll be fine. In the meantime, I have an idea. I'm going to check it out."

McEwen nodded wearily and Steve left the office. Downstairs he ran into additional men from headquarters just arriving. "Gil's up in Lowell's office," Steve informed them and then headed for the side door and his parked roadster.

CHAPTER 3

Steve drove to an all-night pharmacy a few blocks away. He parked out front and walked in, looking for a telephone. On the way to the booth in the back, his eyes lit on a rack of books. One of them read: "Everyday Astrology: A Searchlight on Your Personality" by Thomas Flint. Steve picked up the booklet and flipped through it. There were those strange symbols again. He skimmed through a few pages and found that symbol he'd seen in Lowell's journal — two concave arcs back to back with a line running through them. It was the symbol representing the astrological sign of Pisces, the fish. Quickly, he scanned the paragraph and nodded slightly to himself. His glance flickered to another booklet, which he pulled from the rack. Steve paid for both booklets and then, rolling them slightly, slipped them into the same pocket as Sandy Lowell's "Ephemeris for 1936." He walked briskly to the phone booth at the back of the shop and dialed a number known only to three people. The call was picked up immediately. "Angel?"

At the other end of the line, Dargan's voice sounded tight, stressed. "Boss! Listen, Sue is in a bad way. I haven't let her answer the phone, like you said not to. But she's tried to walk out of here twice. I had to tie her up, Boss! It was the only way to keep her here. She was talking about wanting to see the moon. I...I didn't think she was talking about you, Boss. I'm not sure what she wanted, but I didn't let her go."

Steve's heart sank. "You did the right thing, Angel. I'm coming over right now; I'll be there in a few minutes." Sue's drugged compulsions were getting stronger. How did datura work anyway? Could the mysterious Nine Spheres have left some kind of suggestion in her mind when she was unconscious? Or was she obsessed with the moon because her fiancé was the Moon Man? Steve Thatcher climbed into his roadster and kicked the motor into gear. As the car spurted away from the curb, his gaze turned upwards to the tower of the Metropolitan Building. The clock read twelve-thirty. Eight hours, at least, before the lab reports came back. His gloved hands clenched around the steering wheel as he drove to Dargan's hideout.

Sue was stretched out on the couch, a light wool coverlet tucked in around her. Steve Thatcher sat at the dining table with Ned Dargan, examining various pamphlets and ledgers. Pads of paper and pencils were scattered across the messy tabletop. In the bungalow's coat closet was the bag containing the cash from Lowell's safe. Dargan would distribute it to the fire-displaced needy as soon as Steve returned Sue to Doctor Reinhold's care in the morning.

Steve studied the array of pamphlets spread out before him — the "Farmer's Almanac," the "Ephemeris for 1936," and "Everyday Astrology." He glanced quickly at the clock. It was just past 1:30. He turned back to the papers in front of him and the strange symbols danced before his tired eyes, changing shape and blurring. Steve rubbed his eyes and took a sip of tepid coffee. He knew the astrological code was the key to finding the Nine Spheres. Lowell's ledgers had cryptic notes mentioning six of them—Mercury, Mars, Luna, Venus, Uranus, Jupiter, and the Sun. "Mercury" was one of the two men that had held Sue hostage. Mercury seemed to be a key piece. The glyph for Mercury was in all the messages. Symbolically, Mercury was a cosmic messenger, so it seemed to make sense that he was their director. According to the astrological code, "Mercury" would have been born either under the Sun signs of Gemini or Virgo, meaning the beginning of summer or the early fall. Not that those facts helped him in the least.

Across the table, Dargan was creating a chart at Steve's direction. The table showed the astrological symbols, the planets they represented, and times and dates of the Nine Spheres' robberies, as well as the date and time of Sue's kidnapping. The ex-pug with the cauliflower ear frowned in intense concentration. His tongue stuck out slightly from one corner of his mouth as he carefully wrote down the strange symbols. He put down his pencil and pushed another completed sheet across the table at Steve. Steve took it and looked for commonalities down the columns of glyphs. Although the sign for Mercury appeared more than the others, there was another symbol that showed up as frequently—it was similar to the letter "m" with an arrow heading upward from the bottom. He checked the list; it was the symbol for Scorpio. Steve rubbed his chin and thought. Scorpio was supposed to be a sign that liked to keep secrets, maybe this was their leader. He put down the paper and made a sound of frustration. This was impossible!

On the couch, Sue moaned in her sleep and both men looked up anxiously. Sue was muttering, seeming to struggle in her sleep. Suddenly, she made a startled cry and bolted awake, sitting up with wide, startled eyes. "Where...am I?" she cried. Her complexion was pasty and stress lines showed at the edges of her fine mouth.

Steve rushed to her side. "You're at Angel's hideaway. Don't you remember?"

Sue shook her head blankly. "I ... I don't remember. Were we going to see a spiritualist? Or did we? Oh Steve, my mind's all mixed up!"

He sat beside her on the couch and took her hand. "It's alright, darling. Just calm down and maybe you'll remember."

"I can't, I can't!" She got a strange look on her face. "Has the moon risen yet, Steve?" Her strained voice was tinged with desperation.

"I think so. Let me look." He went to the window and pulled back the curtains. Outside, cold moonlight brightened the street. He turned back to her. "It's up...why?"

She stood, catching the couch's arm with one shaky hand. "It's nothing, I just...wondered." Sue glanced at her purse and hat on the table. She picked up the purse, gazing at it thoughtfully for a moment. Then her gaze shifted to the hat. She seemed unsure, but finally picked it up as well. As Sue walked towards the powder room, her face had an oddly blank look.

"Sue?"

Her expression regained some clarity. "I'm fine, darling. I just want to freshen up my face. The flowers on my hat were crushed when you put it down. I can fix them up with a bit of reshaping. Don't worry." She smiled briefly then closed the powder room door.

As soon as she'd closed the door, Dargan said: "I don't like the look of this, Boss. Are you sure we shouldn't get her to a doctor tonight?"

"Even if we did take her to another doctor, they'd still have to check her blood, and that would take time. Better we keep her comfortable here until the lab results are back in the morning."

The two men returned to work.

A few minutes passed and Steve glanced at the closed powder room door. He looked at Dargan, who returned his worried glance. Steve got up and knocked. "Sue, honey, are you alright?"

No answer.

"Sue? Sue!" He tried the handle, and it turned. The room was empty and the window, wide open. He cursed and leaned out of the ground story window. Sue McEwen was nowhere in sight!

Sue walked briskly down the street, heels clicking on the pavement. She did not have her coat and it was chilly, but she did not feel the cold. All she knew was that she had to get to Police Headquarters before the moon set. The risen quarter moon seemed to guide her steps, telling her what to do. The silvery moon—there was something so comforting about it, so familiar. She hurried along the quiet residential streets, eyes vague. Periodically, she'd glance upwards and a smile would grace her red lips. After walking for more than a mile, a cruising police car caught her slight figure in their headlights. The roadster pulled over and a blue-coated policeman leaned out the window and asked: "Is there a problem, Miss?" But then he got a better look at her face. "Miss McEwen! What are you doing out here in the middle of the night?"

Sue turned to him and, after a moment, smiled. "It's Kyle McDonough, isn't it?"

"Yes, Miss. Can we give you a lift somewhere?"

"I'd love a ride to Police Headquarters."

McDonough glanced over at his partner behind the wheel. "Okay, Bob?"

Bob Freeman nodded. "If we didn't, I wouldn't want to hear what McEwen would say about it! Hop in, Miss."

McDonough got out and helped Sue into the car. "What are you doing out here in the middle of the night, Miss McEwen?"

Sue looked wistful. "Just looking at the moon."

As the patrol car kicked into gear, McDonough asked: "Been out drinking tonight, Miss McEwen?"

"Oh no, I'm as sober as they come. Hurry, please."

The patrolmen glanced at each other as Sue gazed dreamily out the window.

Steve Thatcher and Ned Dargan searched the neighboring streets on foot. At two in the morning, the neighborhood was quiet. The beams from their penlights moved across the sidewalks and streets in nervous stabs. Af-ter a few minutes, they reconvened and compared notes. Clearly, Sue had left the neighborhood, but under her own power? That was yet to be seen.

"Where could she go, Boss?" Dargan wondered. The ex-pug with no neck and the cauliflower ear looked around in distress.

Thatcher wondered the same. And more, who had put that suggestion in her head? There was no way the Nine Spheres could have contacted her at Dargan's hideout. But something was triggering the chemicals in her system. Could the meeting with Madame Mystery have been the catalyst for her strange behavior?

"We need to find her," he told Dargan. "Get your car and head west. I'll go east. She can't have gotten that far." The ex-pug headed for the bungalow's garage while Steve Thatcher slipped behind the wheel of his own roadster and turned the engine over. The purring engine slipped smoothly into gear. As he rolled down the street, he was haunted by the thought that Sue had become obsessed with the moon. What did that mean?

Sandy Lowell, secretly Neptune of the Nine Spheres, was filling out paperwork at Police Headquarters when Sue arrived in the company of the two patrolmen. She stopped to speak with the desk sergeant on the way in. When Lowell saw her, an excited gasp escaped his lips. Mercury had lost track of her, but here she was. He noted the girl looked somewhat vague and glassy-eyed. The drug was working on her, all right! If he could just get her alone for a moment, he could implant the post-hypnotic suggestion that would get them their ransom money. And he needed that money! His safe had been cleaned out tonight and his gambling debts needed to be paid. Mercury had mentioned something about the Moon Man on the phone. Well, of course, he was involved! The famous crook had robbed him not once, but twice!

Sue McEwen walked into the room and looked around vaguely. She turned back to the desk sergeant. "Has Dad gone home?"

"Yes, Miss. The night shift is on now. I can have one of the boys give you a lift home if you want."

Sue waved a hand. "That's alright. I might as well stay here for the rest of the night; I need to be here in the morning, anyway. I'll rest on the couch in Dad's office." She went into the office that Gil McEwen shared with the Chief of Police, Steve Thatcher's father, Peter Thatcher. She sat down.

Sandy Lowell finished his paperwork and picked up the sheets. His gaze raked the room, observing that only one of the skeleton crew was in the squad room at that moment. He waited until the detective left the room then hurried to McEwen's office and slipped inside.

Sue looked up from the magazine she was reading. "Why Mr. Lowell! What are you doing here?"

He looked chagrinned. "My store was robbed tonight, for a second time! It was the Moon Man. They almost caught him, but he slipped away."

Sue's eyes widened and her gaze became sharper. "I had no idea," she whispered. Then she frowned, as if trying to remember something important. From her expression, it was clear she couldn't lay hold of the missing thought. Her gaze became vague once more.

"Miss McEwen, I'd like to talk with you for a moment, if I could."

"Of course, Mr. Lowell."

Sandy Lowell shut the office door. "Miss McEwen, I want you to listen very carefully..."

A few minutes later, he walked out of Gil McEwen's office. Behind him, Sue was deeply asleep on the couch. Lowell deposited his sworn-out complaint

with the desk sergeant, then hurried down the old wooden stairs and out of Police Headquarters.

CHAPTER 4

It was now 3:00 AM and Steve Thatcher was no closer to finding Sue. Thatcher and Dargan had crossed and crisscrossed the area around Dargan's hideaway, but had found nothing. They concluded she must have gotten a lift or taken a bus. But to where?

In desperation, Steve called headquarters to initiate a wider search. Officer Riley, the night switchboard operator, answered.

"Riley, this is Steve. I need to put out an all points for Sue McEwen. I'll be down there in—"

Riley interrupted: "What for, Steve? She's right here."

"What! When did she get there?"

"About an hour ago. A couple of the boys brought her in."

"Is she okay...?"

"Sure, Steve. You want to talk to—"

The discordant noises of a huge rending crash sounded behind Riley's voice. "Holy Hannah!" Riley cried. "That was inside headquarters!"

Steve started to sweat. "Riley, what's happening?"

"An explosion, Steve! Right here in headquarters...I have to clear the line..."

"I'll be right there. Call Gil and my Dad!" Steve hung up the phone and grabbed his overcoat. "Angel, Sue's at headquarters and there's been an explosion. I'm going."

"What can I do, Boss?"

Steve scooped up his hat from the chair where he'd dropped it. "It'll be risky, Angel."

"I don't care. Sue needs our help." Dargan's expression showed determination and no fear. The ex-pug reached for his jacket.

"Alright, Angel. You lie low somewhere near headquarters and keep an eye out for her. I don't want her slipping by us again."

"Right, Boss! I'll be there."

Thatcher nodded. "Come on!" They left the bungalow together, then split up, each to his own car.

Police Headquarters was in an uproar. An explosion had gone off in Gil McEwen's office. The safe door had been blown open. The ransom money, and Sue, were nowhere to be found. It appeared that a single stick of dynamite had been attached to the safe door. The office was still mostly intact except that the blast had also blown upwards and the ceiling now contained a two-foot, charred hole. They quickly discovered that the arms locker had been broken into. The strong box containing explosives had been rifled.

Gil McEwen arrived at approximately the same time as Steve Thatcher. "By damn!" McEwen swore as he took in his ruptured office. "Who the hell marched in here and blew up the safe?" His voice threatened mayhem for the night staff. "Ryan, get in here!" he roared.

Sergeant Ryan, a big tough veteran cop, nonetheless looked queasy as he bolted into the shattered office. Thatcher was right behind him.

"Well? Well!" McEwen demanded. The craggy-faced man hunter scowled his rage as he rounded on the bewildered desk sergeant. "Did you slip out for dinner and a movie last night? Well, did you?" McEwen's face was the color of raw beef.

Ryan spread his hands, looking at once apologetic and disorientated. "Honestly, Gil. I don't know how this could have happened. There was nothing at all going on last night. The only thing that happened was that Sandy Lowell came in to swear out a complaint, but he left forty minutes ago."

A dark scowl overshadowed McEwen's face. "So the safe blew up and then robbed itself, did it?"

Ryan shook his head, devastated. He was about to protest again when Thatcher interrupted. "Where's Sue?" he demanded, hotly.

"She was here? You were supposed to be watching her, Steve!"

"Sue's had weird hallucinations all night. She got away from me and I've been looking for her everywhere."

"That's right, Gil," Ryan said. "Two of the boys picked her up. They found her wandering the streets. She was resting in your office."

McEwen chewed his cigar. "Riley!" The blue-coated switchboard man came running. "Call the Doc. I want him here on the double. Ryan, I want this safe fingerprinted." After the two policemen had left the office, Gil rubbed his eyes. Like Steve, he hadn't slept. "Steve, do you think they got to her?" He sounded as if he already knew the answer. "Sue could have done this. She knows how to get into the arms locker and she knows something about explosives, too. I taught her myself. How did they get to her...? How?"

"Gil, Sandy Lowell was here at the same time as Sue. He could have planted a post-hypnotic suggestion in her mind. She's been having hallucinations, a suggestion like that could have triggered her to do this."

"You think Lowell's one of the Nine Spheres?"

"I do. Have you ever heard of the science of Astrology?"

"You mean fortune telling?"

Thatcher nodded. "I've been working out a cypher for their communications code. They use the names of the planets to identify themselves. More than that, they design horoscopes to figure out the best time to plan their thefts. Sandy Lowell is one of them, I think he's Neptune. The ringleader is a chap they call

Mercury. I think he's Sampson Stark, head of Bingo Tires."

"So Sue's likely to take the loot to one of them."

"That's what I think, too."

McEwen mashed the hat back down onto his head. He was still wearing his coat. He glanced at the wall clock. "I'm going to get Lowell. Sampson Stark, too. It's nearly 5:30 now, they'll still be home. You coming, Steve?"

Steve Thatcher nodded.

Both men were well aware that the Nine Sphere's victims didn't survive their crimes. And Sue was on her way to them with the ransom money.

Ned Dargan was watching Police Headquarters from the shadows of a doorway two blocks away. His cap was pulled down over his eyes and he was pressed back as far as he could against the door behind him. False dawn was pinking the sky as a police roadster pulled out of the garage and headed slowly down the street towards him. The car wove unsteadily, as if driven by a drunkard. As the car rolled by, Dargan saw Sue behind the wheel. Her hands were clamped around the steering wheel and she was squinting at the street ahead as if having trouble seeing it.

Dargan dashed from his hiding place. "Sue!" he cried, waving his arms for good measure.

The car juddered to an abrupt stop. Sue rolled down the window. Her expression showed confusion and fear. "Angel, is it you?"

Dargan stepped onto the running board. "It's me, Sue. You don't look so good. Want me to take you somewhere?" He noticed a shallow cut on her cheek. The lace collar of her dress was singed.

She nodded. "I'd like that. I'm supposed to take this money," she indicated a bag on the front seat, "to a certain address." Her hands were shaking.

Dargan's heart constricted with pity for the girl. "Shove over, Sue. I'll take you." She slid over to the passenger's side while he slipped behind the wheel. This was one of the greatest risks he'd ever taken—stealing a police car when he was already wanted for a slew of crimes! But he couldn't let Sue drive off by herself. Maybe he could get her to safety before the cops caught up with them.

"Gil, wait!" Sergeant Ryan called as McEwen and Steve Thatcher started down the stairs.

McEwen turned, teeth clamped around his unlighted cigar. "Yeah? What is it?"

The desk sergeant hurried over with two sheets of paper clutched in his hands. "Look at this," he held up one of the pages. "This is the statement Lowell filled out tonight. He lied about his whereabouts the night Sue was snatched. According to this, he'd just returned tonight from a few days out of town. And look, here's the report from that night. See? Right here! You can't be in two places at once. His alibi stinks!"

McEwen grabbed the sheets and read them through. His flinty eyes took on a dangerous glint. "By damn, you're right. He used Stark as his alibi the other night, saying they were out discussing business. He never mentioned a trip out of town. Ryan, I want him picked up for questioning. Keep him here until I get back. I have some questions for Sampson Stark, too." Then McEwen turned and charged down the stairs, Thatcher right beside him.

In the garage beneath headquarters, a blue-coated policeman named Murphy was studying the license plates of the parked police cars. His frowning gaze shifted from the clipboard in his hands to each car in turn. Murphy looked up as the two detectives entered the garage. "Lieutenant, it looks like Car 15 is missing."

"What!" McEwen roared.

Steve Thatcher felt his throat constrict. "When?" He rasped.

"I'm not too sure, Steve. It must have been taken sometime in the last hour. That's when I took over from Dobbs. I looked at the reports and Car 15 is supposed to be here."

McEwen's face paled. "Have Riley put out a radio alert for Car 15. I want it detained. No shooting, understand?"

"Sure, Lieutenant. I'll tell him."

McEwen and Thatcher hurried to one of the police roadsters. "God Steve, what if she's gone completely off the rails?"

Thatcher made a grim mouth. "We can't think about that right now, Gil. We have to figure out where she went." He stopped with his hand on the door handle. "I'm an idiot! All those figures, I forgot. Look Gil, that cypher I was working out tonight...one of the coded messages was about the 30th—that's today! I didn't understand all of it, but there was something about the morning star, Venus, and the Dog Star, Sirius. When they come together, something is supposed to happen."

"That sounds like a bunch of baloney," Gill said while sliding into the car. "But you say Sampson Stark's involved, and that's enough for me. You coming?"

Thatcher hesitated. "There may be something else in my cypher that can help us. The notes are in my car. I'll follow you."

Gil McEwen grunted and started the engine.

Steve Thatcher's mind was whirling. He slipped into his own car and his gaze shifted to the rubber-banded accordion folder on the passenger's seat. He grabbed the folder and tore free the band then pulled forth a sheaf of papers. He began flipping through them until he found the one he was looking for. One of the messages in Sandy Low-

ell's ledgers read as follows: "When the Morning Star and the Dog Star give salutation to the sun, it's a fortuitous moment for wealth. It was followed by today's date and a few astrological symbols. Also the notation, "60 feet, north by northwest corner." It sounded like so much nonsense. But was it?

He started the engine and pulled away from the curb. Certain facts spun in his head, looking for a way to mesh. How did Sampson Stark, Bingo Tires, dog star, and Mercury fit together? He still had the matchbook in his pocket. He pulled it out and looked at the small cardboard box. The logo showed a sitting dog with a rilled collar. There was a billboard on the roof of the Bingo Tires building with the same image. It was a big six story building—about 60 feet. The small box rattled in his hand. At a stoplight, he pushed the box open and saw the tie tack. He noted that the head of the pin showed a star. When the light changed, he gunned the motor. He knew where Sue was going.

Dargan drove carefully, not wanting to draw unwanted attention. His neck was sweat-dampened even in the early morning chill. "Sue, how about I drive you back to the bungalow? You can call the Boss and he can come and pick you up there. How about it?"

Her eyes widened with fear. "No! No, I can't do that. You see, it's critically important I deliver this bag of money at just the right time." She glanced at her watch, hands visibly shaking. "We still have t...time. Please h...hurry, Angel."

Dargan glanced at the girl. She was staring straight ahead, hands clasped around the bag filled with her own ransom. He muttered, "Oh God."

The police radio crackled to life. "Calling all cars, calling all cars. Be on the look-out for Car Number 15, it has been stolen. Repeat, Car 15 has been stolen.

Orders from McEwen, if seen, the car is to be detained, but no violent action taken. Repeat, locate the car, but do not take any violent action." Then the message repeated.

Dargan felt his stomach drop into his shoes. He couldn't stay on the streets now. But Sue, what would she do if he didn't take her where she wanted to go? The address she'd given him was still ten minutes away, plenty of time for a police car to find them. "Sue, we have to get out of this car before the police find us." He started to turn onto a side street.

"Please don't do that, Angel." Suddenly Sue was pointing a small caliber handgun at him. She must have taken it out of the ransom bag which was now opened in her lap. "We have to get to that address before 6:00." In the rising light, Dargan could see that her eyes were glassy. A vein jumped in her white throat.

Now he had no choice. He pressed down on the gas and the police car sped forward.

Thatcher's car slewed to a stop in front of the Bingo Tires building. Early morning workers were hurrying to the front door in ones and twos, ready for the workday to begin. Steve got out of his car and gazed upwards. The building's roof seemed quiet, although it was hard to tell from the street. He went to the rumble compartment and unlocked it. From it, he drew the case containing the regalia of the Moon Man. Once more locking the compartment, he entered the building. Inside, he consulted the list of the departments and offices. Sampson Stark's offices were on the fifth floor. Next, he looked for a department that might not be tenanted at this early hour. His gaze settled on Literature Storage on the fourth floor and his mouth quirked. Steve hurried to the elevator and asked the operator to take him to the fourth floor. Once there, he headed for office 412. The door was unlocked. Inside were orderly stacks of printed literature in cubbies and bookcases. There was a desk in the center, currently unoccupied. Quickly, he shut and locked the door. Settling his bag on the table, he drew out the precious silver sphere swaddled in the black robe. He set the sphere down and shrugged the robe over his shoulders. Next, he drew on a pair of black gloves. Finally, he settled the silver globe on his shoulders and affixed the catches securing it in place. Steve Thatcher was gone and the Moon Man had returned! He hid the bag inside a closet at the rear of the office, then unlocked the door. Peering out, he saw the hall was quiet. Then the living phantom with the head of silver glided silently up to the stairs to the sixth floor. There, the stairs ended. He opened the door and peered out into the hall. He waited, breath held, as two chatting workers exited the elevator and disappeared into an office. He gazed both ways, noting a second, smaller stairway at the end of the hall. Moving quickly, the Moon Man glided to the end of the hall and slipped into the second stairwell. In a moment he was up the flight and facing a locked door. Withdrawing a packet of skeleton keys from a pocket under his robe, he tried first one key and then another. The fourth key fit the lock. The door opened, and he was faced with the legs of a giant billboard. He considered the angle of the building, then hurried to the northwest corner. He drew a pistol from under his robe and waited.

Sampson Stark had come in early, waiting for the inevitable. He glanced at the expensive brass clock on his desk. It was now five forty-five. Any time now, he expected to hear the wail of police sirens and see the flashing of lights. They'd find Sue McEwen's crumpled body on the street beside his building, an apparent suicide. Neptune and Mars would have the cash, and they'd hand it over to Luna for distribution to the rest of the gang. But something was worrying him. This was not the ideal day for the girl's murder. He got up and walked to a coat stand and picked up the briefcase standing beside it. He brought the case back to his desk and took a tiny key from his pocket. He unlocked the case and unsnapped the hasps. Inside was a pile of papers and a few small books. He flipped open one of the books and quickly consulted one table and then another. His mouth tightened and his expression took on a look of consternation. Stark returned the book to the briefcase and pulled forth a pad of paper. The surface was covered with esoteric symbols arranged in circular shapes as well as in carefully constructed charts. At the bottom of each page were several columns written in shorthand. Stark rubbed his chin while gazing at a series of notations. Taken together, the messages meant: *the daylight brings prosperity, but the night heralds dangerous exploits.* A feeling of unease flitted through him. As long as the Morning Star was gone from the sky, they'd succeed. If not ... he glanced again at the desk clock. Sue McEwen must fall to her death before dawn!

Police Car 15 dashed up Great City's main boulevard. Dargan realized abruptly that the address Sue wanted was the Bingo Tires building. As the huge square edifice hove into view, Sue gazed upwards and gave a little gasp. Her face took on a look of eager excitement. "There it is!" She exclaimed in delight. She glanced hurriedly at her strap watch. "I still have time."

"What are you going to do, Sue?" The ex-pug with the cauliflower ear knew he had to go with her to wherever it was. He wouldn't abandon her, not for nothing! If only there was a way to let Steve know where they were! Suddenly, he saw a way. On the dashboard in front of Sue was the police radio. But if they let on where they were....Sue was sitting at the edge of her seat, eyes shining as she glanced up at the image of the sitting dog with the rilled collar.

Dargan knew what he had to do. "Sue, I want you to call Steve on the police radio. You have to tell him where you are."

"Tell...Steve?" Her voice caught. She looked suddenly of two minds. The girl rubbed her eyes and shook her head slightly. She glanced at Dargan, and her eyes looked strange. "Angel, why are we here?" Her voice was faint and

wretched. "What's happening to me?"

Angel reached over and patted her hand. "It'll be okay, Sue. Just let Steve know where you are."

She nodded mechanically and reached for the radio receiver. She had it in her hand when police sirens started wailing from two different directions. Dargan gunned the motor and the police car spurted forwards. Sue was looking through the window, eyes tracking a police car with a red light flashing hectically. "They're getting closer..." Calmly, almost mechanically, she rolled down the window and raised the small pistol.

"Sue, you can't!" Dargan pulled the wheel over hard and the big car swerved. Sue was thrown against the passenger door. The pistol dropped, clattering into the floor well. As she reached for it, Dargan pulled the car to an abrupt stop. He gambled that the compulsion to deliver the money was stronger than her desire to shoot. "Come on, Sue! It's almost six o'clock!" He opened the driver's door, then grabbed her hand, pulling her from the car. Her free hand grasped the handle of the bag containing the ransom money. The two sprinted across the sidewalk and into the Bingo Tires building as two police cars, with lights flashing and sirens wailing, zoomed up the street. Her pistol remained on floor of the police car.

Inside the building, Dargan glanced around nervously. When he saw no security guard in the lobby, he let go a breath. Sue pulled his hand, dragging him towards the elevator. The attendant opened the door and Sue ordered him to take them up to the sixth floor. As the door closed, a pair of blue-coated policemen entered the building. They looked around and didn't quite see them as the elevator door closed. Sue glanced furtively to the left and right, even in the elevator where there was nothing to see. As they ascended, she started to visibly shake. Her face was an unhealthy shade and her breathing was ragged.

"Sue, are you alright?"

She gasped and fanned her face with one hand. "It's so hot in here," she muttered. Weakly, she leaned back against the wall of the elevator.

They exited at the sixth floor and Sue staggered, a hand pressed to her heart. Dargan moved in to help her but she shook her head. After a few seconds she walked unsteadily to a smaller set of stairs leading to the roof. Angel knew they only had a few minutes before the police got here. If they caught him, it would mean the electric chair, but that didn't deter him. He'd stick with Sue as long as her life was in danger.

The Moon Man surveyed the roof from his position behind one of the billboard's massive supports. A nervous feeling struck him as the sky began to lighten. The Moon Man's domain was dark of night; he was never seen during daylight. And yet he knew he had to remain until this strange crime reached its conclusion. The sounds of police sirens grew louder until they shrieked from the street directly below. Glancing over the edge of the roof, the vigilante with the head of silver saw two police roadsters with lights flashing pull up in front of the building. They stopped behind another police car already parked at a haphazard angle. That car! From his vantage point, he could easily see the number printed large on the roof.... fifteen! He glanced at his strap watch. Nearly six o'clock now. Nervously, his fingers touched the pamphlet stuffed into his pocket under the robe. The Nine Spheres and their weird mysticism—they played by a stiff rulebook. If so, did they anticipate his plans? The sounds of a creaky door being pushed open caused his fingers to drop away from the booklet. He moved back into the shadowy darkness behind the leg of the billboard.

The roof stairs let out into a small triangular hut. The door of the hut opened and a big, roughneck emerged. He wore workmen's coveralls and a cap pulled down over his shaggy brows. A jutting jaw gave him a truly brutish appearance. He looked around briefly before beckoning to someone behind him. Another man exited onto the roof. The second man wore an expensive topcoat with a fur collar. The bigger man looked at his watch and said brusquely: "The cops are coming up. What do we do?"

The other man waved negation with a gloved hand. "We've done nothing wrong. We're not even trespassing. Relax. We'll even try to stop her from jumping and if we fail, who can blame us for trying?" He laughed nastily. "We'll be heroes. Come on, Mars. We need to get into position."

The Moon Man recognized that voice— it was Sandy Lowell, owner of Lowell's Department store and Neptune of the Nine Spheres! Silently, he followed the two men across the roof.

A moment or two later, the door to the roof stairs opened again, this time disgorging Sue McEwen and Ned Dargan. Sue carried a satchel in one hand. Before she'd taken three steps, Dargan ducked in front of her, arms held wide. "Sue, stop! Please. You don't know what you're doing. The cops will be here in a minute. You can give them back the money and everything will be jake. Come on, Sue! Stop!" He grabbed her arm.

"Let me go!" She shrieked and tried to shake off Dargan's restraining hand, but the ex-pug would not give way.

As they struggled, Mars came striding across the roof. The brute-faced Mars grabbed one of Dargan's arms and spun him around to face him. "You heard the lady, punk. Get outta the way!" He drew back an arm and aimed a hairy fist at Dargan's face.

Angel blocked the blow with his forearm and let fly a blow of his own. He clipped Mars' ear and the other man grunted, then snarled. The two men traded blows, hard-knuckled fists smashing into the other's head and body. As they fought, Sue McEwen stole away with the ransom money. Had she been in her right mind, she would never have abandoned such a true friend as Ned Dargan, but Sue was not in her right mind. Her feverish eyes scanned the area, looking for something half seen in the pre-dawn light. Tension showed in the stiffness of her spine, the thin line of her taut mouth. When Sandy Lowell stepped forward, the tension vanished from Sue's face. She held out the bag with an eager thrust. "Here it is!"

The Moon Man stepped out from behind one of the billboard's supports. He pointed a pistol at Lowell. "Mr. Lowell, step back. Miss McEwen, put the bag down, if you please."

Sandy Lowell raised his hands and backed up a step. Sue turned and stared at the silver-headed phantom. On her face was a look of utter dread. Her voice was hoarse with despair as she said: "I...I can't! Oh, I can't stop! You don't understand. Please, St..." She gasped in horror at her near-blunder; a mistake which would have cost them both dearly. Her hand flew to her mouth while her eyes pleaded for forbearance. Tears misted her sight. "I can't!" She tossed the bag of money at Sandy Lowell's feet. "Take it and let me go!"

In a lightning swift movement, Lowell grabbed Sue's arm and pulled her in front of him. "Pick up that bag," he demanded of the girl. "Now!" As she reached forward, he drew a pistol and pointed it at her head, meanwhile pulling her back against him.

The Moon Man took a step forward. "Stop! Drop your gun or I shoot!"

The Moon Man's silvery head lowered slightly, as if in consternation. "The police are coming," he said. "I wouldn't want to be holding a gun at Miss McEwen's head when her father arrives."

Lowell swallowed visibly and his gaze flickered to the small triangular hut housing the top of the stairs to the roof. A few feet in front of it, Mars of the Nine Spheres lay prone, unconscious. Ned Dargan was striding towards them, wearing a grim expression and bloodied knuckles. After a moment of hesitation, Lowell thrust Sue violently away from him. She stumbled badly and nearly fell as Lowell bolted. The Moon Man caught her. The bag with the ransom money fell and spilled open, a few loose bills wafting gently in the pre-dawn air.

The phantom with the head of silver settled Sue back onto her feet. "Sue, stay here. Will you do that?"

She nodded heavily, slowly. He slipped something into her shaking hand. "Put this on," he said then gestured for Dargan to follow him. As the two men sprinted after Sandy Lowell, Sue looked down. In her palm rested a tiny pin with the head of a star. She fixed it to her dress, then waited as dawn brightened the horizon. Automatically, she picked up the fallen bills and stuffed them back into the bag, then fastened the catch. She looked briefly in the direction the Moon Man and Dargan had gone, then dragged her attention back to the exit of the roof stairs. The bag containing the ransom money sat at her feet.

Sandy Lowell, Neptune of the Nine Spheres, ran to the far northwest corner of the roof with the Moon Man and Dargan hot on his heels. A scaffold had been erected against that side of the building where brickwork was under obvious repair. Lowell climbed out onto the scaffold and grabbed a pullied rope. The Moon Man and Dargan arrived in time to see the scaffold began to lower. They leaped down onto the platform together.

Lowell was reaching for his gat when the Moon Man clipped his chin with a well-thrown punch. Lowell stumbled back towards the edge of the planking, wind-milling to keep from plunging over the side. The Moon Man grabbed his coat front and pulled him in close. "Did it ever occur to you that the astrology of the day might also include me?" He asked in a low voice.

Lowell started, genuinely frightened now, and once more fumbled for his gun. The Moon Man hit him again and Sandy Lowell collapsed against the grip on his overcoat. The Moon Man dropped him to the boards, then unwound a piece of jute cord from one of the guard planks. Tying Lowell's hands securely, he grasped the pullied rope. "Lend a hand, Angel. We're going to see Sampson Stark."

As the scaffold descended, the triangular hut on the roof disgorged a mob of police, Gil McEwen in the lead. Their first sight was of the brutish Mars lying unconscious a few feet in front of the door. Then the ace manhunter caught sight of his daughter standing a few yards away with the ransom money at her feet. "Sue! Oh God, Sue, are you all right?" He rushed forward while calling out, "handcuff that hood," to the blue-coated policemen behind him.

The girl smiled wanly. "I'm okay, Dad. I'm so sorry about all this mess. I truly am!" She fell into her father's arms and sobbed as the tension of the past few hours released.

Gil McEwen patted her back. "It's alright now, Sue. Everything's going to be okay. What the hell happened up here?"

Sue didn't trust herself to keep from blurting out certain things which must remain secret so she simply said, "I had to bring them the ransom money. That man over there is one of them. Sandy Lowell, escaped." McEwen glanced over his shoulder at the fallen Mars.

"How did you...?"

"I didn't, Dad. It was the Moon Man."

"By damn! I knew that crook was involved somehow!"

"No...he...saved me."

McEwen made a grunting sound which served as an indeterminate reply. "Where did he go, Sue?"

"I...I didn't see," she lied. "Dad, I'm not feeling very well. Do you think you can..." and then the exhausted girl fainted in his arms.

"You there!" he hollered at one of the blue-coated policemen nearby. "Call headquarters and get Doctor Reinhold over here, pronto. If he's not in yet, have the switchboard call him at home." Then he gestured with his free hand to one of his detectives, Frank Packer, who'd come with him. "Frank, stay with Sue until Doc gets here. I'm going after Sandy Lowell." McEwen put Sue down, leaving her in the detective's care. He sprinted for the stairs, pistol positive grasped tightly in his fist.

The Moon Man and Dargan stopped lowering the scaffold outside the fifth floor windows. The tall casements formed a long row on that side of the building. Through the windows, a corridor was visible with offices directly across the hall. The Moon Man touched a gloved hand to one of the tall glass rectangles and pushed. The window did not give, and there was no way to unlock it from the outside. He turned the pistol in his hand and used the butt against the glass. A spiderweb of cracks ran outward from the impact point, but the pane did not break. The silver sphere that was the Moon Man's head lowered slightly, as if listening. Faintly, he heard shouting from the roof above. He raised the gun again. This time there was a satisfying tinkling sound as the glass cracked. Large pieces fell in jagged slices both inside and out-

side the frame. Quickly, he smashed a hole large enough for a man to climb through. He ducked though the broken pane and Dargan followed. Signaling his companion to silence, the Moon Man glided toward Stark's office.

Outside the door, a brass plate read: "Mr. Sampson Stark, President." He could hear movement inside—a chair squeaking as it rolled across a wooden floor. The Moon Man put a gloved hand on the doorknob and turned.

Sampson Stark was sitting at his desk with an open leather briefcase before him. He snapped the lid shut as the Moon Man and Dargan entered. The tire executive, Mercury of the Nine Spheres, reached for the telephone receiver on his desk.

The Moon Man raised his gun. "Drop your hand away from that phone, Mr. Stark. Now, if you please."

Sampson Stark obeyed, eyes wide. Now he understood the stars' warning. He also knew that... "The girl is safe, isn't she?" He blurted.

He could not see the smile that graced the Moon Man's lips. "The sun has risen, Mr. Stark. Venus is no longer visible in the sky."

Stark's face settled into a sneer, as if gazing at a more successful chess player. "So what happens now?"

The Moon Man kept his gat pointed at Stark's head. "You'll wait here until the police arrive. I suspect they'll have some questions for you. I have a few myself. Tell me about Uranus—Aquarius in your little group. He's the boss, isn't he?"

Stark's face went pale. "How did you find that out?"

"According to the stars, Aquarius is the one who thinks the most widely. He's unpredictable. I want to predict him. Who is he? Come, come Mr. Stark. The police are on their way."

"What's in for me, if I tell you?"

"Perhaps you'll be able to stay out of the gas chamber if there's someone else to blame for the deaths of your victims. Please do not stall, Mr. Stark, I'm in a hurry. Angel, would you be kind enough to bring Mr. Lowell in here, along with another cord?"

Dargan hurried out to the scaffold. He climbed out and hoisted Sandy Lowell's unconscious body onto his shoulder. There were the sounds of more police sirens from the street below. Quickly, he pushed Lowell's body through the broken window, then hurried through himself. He carried Sandy Lowell into Stark's office and put him down on the floor.

A look of fearful regret passed over Stark's features when he saw his partner's unconscious body. "I can't tell you, I wish I could. We all wear masks whenever we meet. Each of us only knows a few of the others—my contacts are Neptune and Mars. Mars was Luna's contact and Venus'. I don't know who the others are, honestly!" He paused, eyes rolling slightly as the sounds of police sirens drifted in through the broken window in the hall. "Alright, there is something else I can tell you. Pluto is our chemist, he's brilliant. He's the one who knew about the drug. Uranus has money; he arrives at our meetings in a fine car, a Duesenberg."

"That's a help, Mr. Stark. Thank you. We'll have to tie you up. I wouldn't want you leaving before McEwen arrives. Angel, if you would be so kind?" The Moon Man removed Stark's briefcase from the desk. Next, he picked up a pen from a stand on the desk and wrote a hasty note. He folded the paper and replaced the handkerchief in the breast pocket of Stark's suit with the note. He stuffed the handkerchief into Stark's mouth. "Good-bye, Mr. Stark." The nighttime phantom and the ex-pug with the cauliflower ear slipped out of the office and shut the door. Early morning light shone through the long rows of windows outside the office. Suddenly, they heard the sounds of heavy footsteps pounding the stairs at the end of the hall.

"Back to the scaffold, quickly!" The Moon Man leaned out of the window and glanced at the street below. The side alley was quiet for the moment. They squeezed out of the broken pane and out onto the scaffold. The Moon Man put Stark's briefcase down on the floor planks and then each man took hold of a rope and pulled so as to lower the scaffold. Before they'd gone an entire storey, a man leaned out of the broken window—McEwen! The ace manhunter raised his gat and the muzzle spat flame. Both men ducked down as hot lead roared past. A bullet tore through one of the ropes holding the scaffold. The line in Dargan's hand whipped free like a fast-moving snake. He cried out as the rope tore out of his hands. The scaffolding creaked and tipped dangerously. The Moon Man, hanging onto the scaffold with one arm, raised his pistol and shot out the glass above McEwen's head. The tall window shattered and a shower of glass erupted over Gil McEwen's head. McEwen raised a hand above his hatted head, then ducked back inside. The dangerously hanging scaffold was now level with the top of the tall fourth floor windows. The Moon Man's pistol blasted again and the window before him shattered. Hanging onto the remaining intact rope he cried: "Angel, jump for it!"

As Dargan leaped for the window, the scaffold swung and the Moon Man felt the remaining rope start to give. He took a careful step towards the shattered window. The change of weight on the boards caused the scaffold to drop, sickeningly, a couple of inches. He grabbed for one of the rails to steady himself. He grasped the window frame as Dargan leaned out with hand extended. The Moon Man knew if he took another step, the rope would part for good. He braced himself and leaped. Dargan grabbed his arms and pulled him inside. His kick off the floorboards was the final insult to the frayed pulley rope. With a vibratory snap, the weakened strands gave way and the scaffold let go. A moment later, there was a crash of splintering wood. The scaffold was now a pile of broken boards in the alley below. Mercury's briefcase had been destroyed along with it.

The Moon Man led the way to an office at the far end of the hall. He listened at the door and then entered, gun drawn. Dargan followed, shutting the door behind him. "Lock it, Angel," the Moon Man's muffled voice instructed. Inside, orderly stacks of advertising materials waited for delivery to clients. As before, the desk was empty. The Moon Man glided to the back of the room and retrieved his case from the closet where he'd left it. He noted that the closet was filled with packing supplies. Hanging on a hook was a coverall. A hand truck stood in one corner. He knew that McEwen was moments away from finding them, but in that moment they still had a chance. "Angel, put on that coverall. I'm going to distract them while you go down the elevator with a stack of boxes."

"Boss, you can't! They'll catch you, easy!"

"Maybe," he said quietly. "Even if they do, you'll get away. Now put it on!"

Reluctantly, Dargan pulled the coverall over his clothes. Acting quickly, the two men loaded the hand truck with boxes. "Take them to the basement, then around to the rear of the building. That's where they shift things up to the street through a small service elevator. At this hour, it'll probably be clear. Go!"

Dargan peered outside the door and saw the hall was empty. He pulled his cap down and pushed out the hand truck, heading for the elevator.

Once he'd gone, the Moon Man loosened the clasps that secured the silver sphere atop his shoulders. Carefully, he lifted it off and set it on a table. He shrugged off his black cloak and removed the black gloves. Wrapping the silvery sphere in the cloak, he placed it into the bag, then added the gloves and closed the clasp. The Moon Man had disappeared into the night and in the light of day, Detective Sergeant Stephen Thatcher had returned. Quickly, he hurried out and to the elevator at the opposite corner of the building from where Dargan had gone.

Shattered glass rained down on Gil McEwen's head. He cursed and spat out his cigar, lest he inhale some of the glass fragments. He pulled back inside while outside the crippled scaffold swung perilously. He shook off his hat and brushed off his shoulders even as he ran for the stairway. Suddenly, there were sounds of a resounding crash. McEwen turned to the hall window and looked down. The scaffold was shattered on the street below. His eyes scanned the wreckage but saw no bodies. Gone! The Moon Man had slipped through his fingers again!

From the offices behind him McEwen heard muffled cries. He shoved open the door and saw Sampson Stark bound to his chair and Sandy Lowell, also tied up, sprawled unconscious on the floor.

"By damn!" McEwen swore and removed a fresh cigar from a case in his pocket. His teeth clenched the cigar as he removed a white folded sheet from Stark's breast pocket.

My dear McEwen,

I leave these two here in good faith. They are two of the Nine Spheres—Sampson Stark plays the part of Mercury—their coordinator, while Sandy Lowell plays the role of Neptune. The man on the roof was Mars; I do not know his real name. Unfortunately, I was not able to discern the others. Only the boss, Uranus, knows the identity of all the gang members. The others only know their own two contacts.

I would not have interfered had they not used Miss McEwen in such a shameful manner. I urge you to contemplate the stars in the capture of this gang, McEwen. It is how they communicate and plan their crimes, through the science of Astrology.

-- M.M.

Gil McEwen bit down angrily on his cigar and scowled.

Thatcher took one of the elevators at the back side of the building. At ground level, he went out a side door and hurried across the street to his roadster. There were police cars everywhere, but, as he'd hoped, the officers were inside the building. He deposited the satchel containing the regalia of the Moon Man inside the rumble compartment of his roadster and locked it securely. Then slid behind the wheel and kicked the motor into action. He drove a few blocks, turned the corner, then drove back along the avenue behind the building, this time parking out front. He got out of the car and hailed one of the cops in the lobby. "Hey Morrison, any action out on the street?"

"Hi Steve. No. Everything's been going on inside the building and on the roof." Quietly, Thatcher let go a breath. They hadn't found Angel, he'd gotten away.

"Where's McEwen?"

"Up in Mr. Stark's office."

Thatcher nodded and took the elevator up.

That evening, Gil McEwen and Steve Thatcher stood at Sue's bedside at Mercy General Hospital. The test results had come back positive for datura poisoning and she'd been given the antidote. Now, a few hours later, the girl seemed well on her way to recovery. That strange otherworldly look was gone from her eyes, and sleep had returned color to her cheeks.

Thatcher caught Sue's hand. "You're going to be alright now, darling," he said, softly.

"Thanks to both of you," she replied. "And I guess, the Moon Man, too."

McEwen made a growling noise in his throat as he brought forth a crumpled letter from his pocket. "Just because that fancy crook helped you, Sue, it doesn't mean I'm not going to get him one day. But I guess, this time, I'm glad he interfered."

"Me too, Dad," Sue said quietly while squeezing Steve's hand. "Me, too."

THE END

ABOUT THE AUTHOR/ILLUSTRATOR

Sara Light-Waller is the daughter of a playwright and a painter. Is it any wonder that she became both writer and illustrator? Add to that several degrees in Anthropology, with specialties in Scientific Illustration, Far Eastern Studies, world mythology, alternative healing, and sound therapies and you get an eclectic artist/healer who doesn't fit well into any box. Sara's published works include genre fiction, children's books, and non-fiction. Her popular weekly podcast, The Rocketeer, reviews pulp stories and provides commentary about pulp era and contemporary fiction topics. She lives in Western Washington, is an avid gardener, and has a growing collection of vintage hats and purses from the 1940s and 50s.

MORE POPULAR ITEMS

ROCKETEER PODCAST

*Your weekly dive into the slickest stories
ever printed on cheap paper!*

**Wednesdays on Substack
lucinarocketeer.substack.com**

LUCINA PRESS BLOG

*Rated among the top pulp
novel blogs on the web!*

lucinapress.com

FLYING PONY STUDIOS

*Real pulp art hand-painted by a
contemporary artist.*

flyingponystudios.com